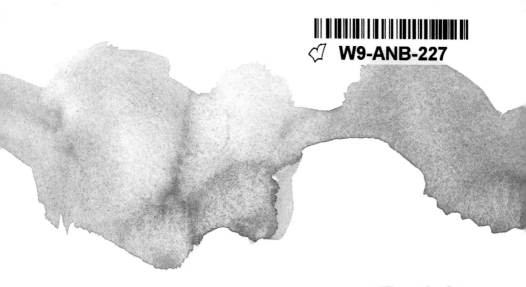

DOOLEY
Makes Friends

Written by Kate Watkins
Illustrated by Kevin Menck

LEVEL  READER

READING LEVEL
1
PRE K - GRADE 1

Dalmatian Press

Dooley was a dinosaur.
He lived in a cave
at the top of a hill.
Most of the time,
Dooley stayed in his cave
to sleep and dream.

But Dooley was lonely.
Sometimes Dooley
came out of his cave.
He looked down into
the valley far below.
Do you know what he saw?

Dooley saw children.
Children playing tag
and hide-and-seek.

They waved at Dooley.
Oh, how Dooley wished
he could play with them.
But would he fit in?

One day, while Dooley
snoozed in his cave,
he heard a sound.
He looked around.

"Hello?" said a voice.
"May I come in?"
It was a child!
A little girl!

"This is for you," said the girl.
She gave Dooley a red flower.
"Do dinosaurs like flowers?"

Dooley nodded.
Yes, yes!

"Do dinosaurs like to play?"

Dooley nodded.
Oh, yes, yes!

"Good!" said the girl.
"I did not know if
I would fit in up here."

The girl and Dooley played.
She rode on Dooley's back.
They played hide-and-seek.

The next day, the girl came back.
And the next day, too.
She read all her favorite
stories to Dooley.
Dooley hummed his favorite
tunes for her.

The other children said:
"How can Rosy play with
a big dinosaur all day?"
They wanted to find out.
Slowly they went up the hill.

But they were a little afraid.
"What if he wants to eat us?"
"What if he steps on me?"
"What if we don't fit in?"

At the top of the hill,
they saw colorful
flowers, tall green trees,
a rocky cave. . .

and a big, friendly smile!
The children smiled, too.
They knew that Dooley
wanted to play.

Wheeee!
The children had so much fun!
This hill was the best playground.
They played tag.
They played hide-and seek.
They swung on rope swings.

Dooley stomped his big foot
to make a hole in the ground.

The children filled it with water.
Now they had a swimming hole.

Dooley loved
his new friends.

Each was different.
Some were tall.
Some were short.
Some were silly.
Some were quiet.
Some liked to swim.
Some liked to swing.
Some liked books.

And everyone
fit right in!